For Denis and Jamie,
who would Eat Pizza every
night if I Let Them!

Henry Holt and Company, *Publishers since 1866*
175 Fifth Avenue, New York, New York 10010
mackids.com

Henry Holt® is a registered trademark of Macmillan Publishing Group, LLC.

Library of Congress Cataloging-in-Publication Data is available.
ISBN 978-1-62779-790-0

Our books may be purchased in bulk for promotional, educational, or business use. Please contact your local bookseller or the Macmillan Corporate and Premium Sales Department at (800) 221-7945 ext. 5442 or by e-mail at MacmillanSpecialMarkets@macmillan.com.

First Edition—2017

Acrylics, collage, Adobe Photoshop, and Adobe Illustrator were used to create the illustrations for this book.
Printed in China by RR Donnelley Asia Printing Solutions Ltd., Dongguan City, Guangdong Province

1 3 5 7 9 10 8 6 4 2

PIZZA DAY

Melissa Iwai

Christy Ottaviano Books
Henry Holt and Company • New York

COFFEE

Today is pizza day.

I get to help Daddy in the garden. Caesar helps too.

The seeds Daddy and
I planted in the spring
have turned into lots of
vegetables and herbs.

This is what we gather from our garden and bring into the house:

Five juicy red tomatoes plucked from the vine.

Four sprigs of basil pinched from the stalk.

Three small carrots pulled
from the ground.

Two round onion bulbs dug up from the earth.

One shiny green pepper clipped
from the plant.

We wash the vegetables and get ready to make pizza.

First we have to make the dough. Daddy measures the yeast, water, oil, salt, and flour, and we pour each one into a big bowl.

I mix it all together with a wooden spoon.
It turns into a big, sticky, squishy lump.

Daddy dumps
the dough onto
a board.

We both knead it
with our hands.

The big, sticky, squishy lump becomes smooth and shiny.

Daddy says we have to let the dough rest for an hour so it can rise. We let it take a little nap while we start the tomato sauce.

"Sweet dreams, Pizza Dough," I whisper.

Daddy chops the tomatoes and carrots and onions we brought in from the garden. Mmmm! It starts to smell yummy in our kitchen as the vegetables and herbs cook in the oil.

The sauce needs to cook for a while so that the vegetables can soften. Now it's time for the sauce to take a little nap. "Sweet dreams, Tomato Sauce," I say.

There are a lot of things to do outdoors while the dough and the *sauce* rest.

We play catch.

We slay some dragons.

We wrestle a wild beast to the ground.
Then it's time to finish making the pizza!

"WAKE UP!" I say as I uncover the dough.
It's grown twice as big! I get to punch it down.
WHAM!

Daddy plops
it onto a baking
sheet and rolls
it into a big circle.
This will be the crust.

"WAKE UP!" I shout again as Daddy uncovers the pan. The sauce is thick and darker red now.

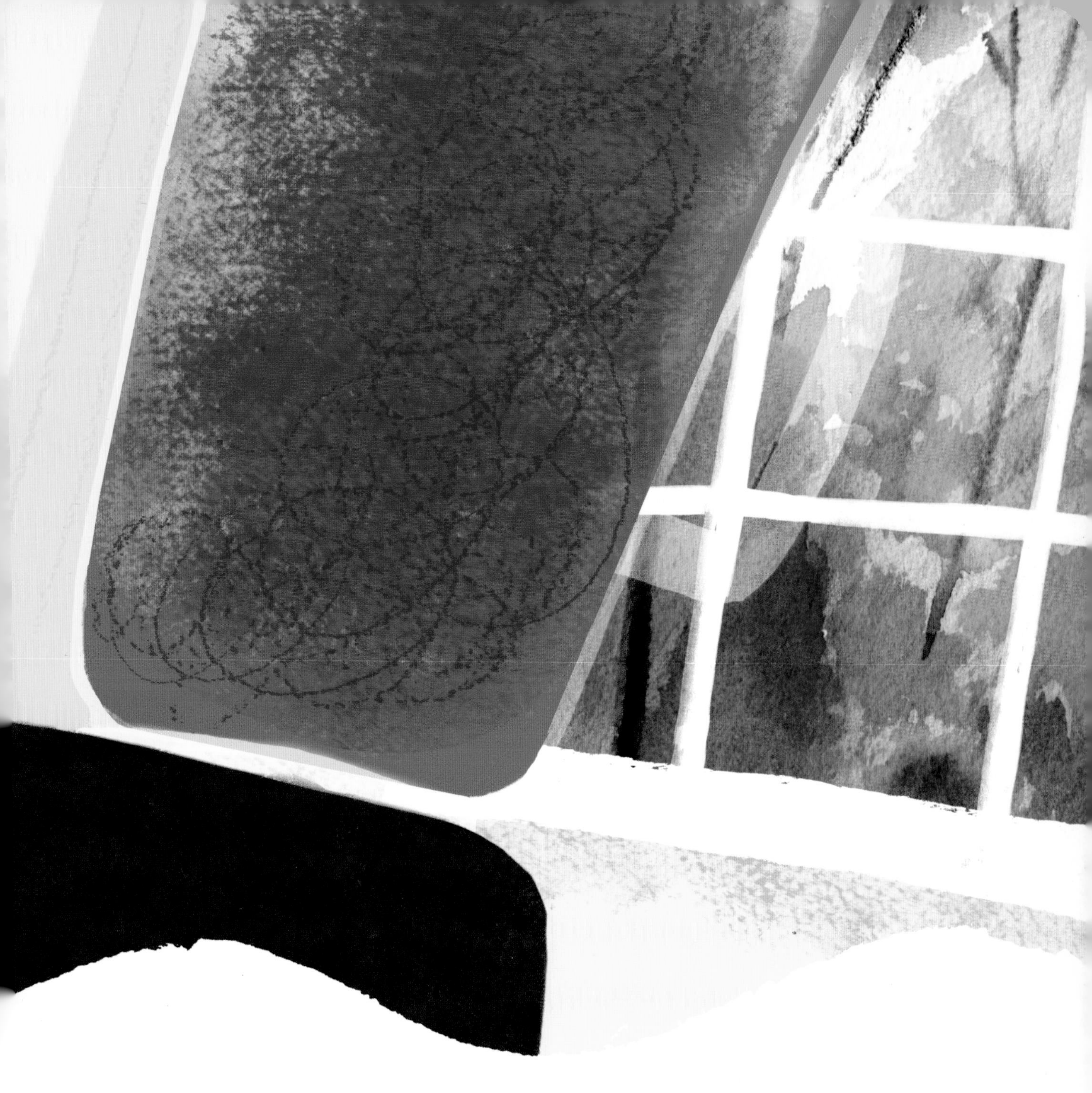

We put it in the *blender*. I push the *button*.
WHIZZZZZ! The *sauce* wakes up.

Now we can put together the pizza!

START:

1. Roll out dough.

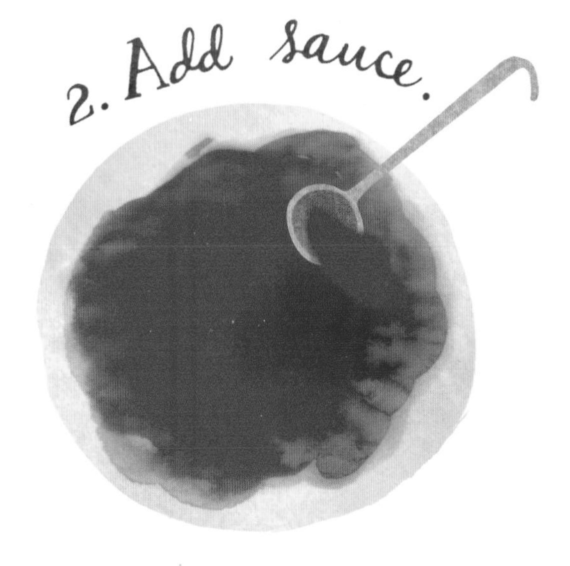

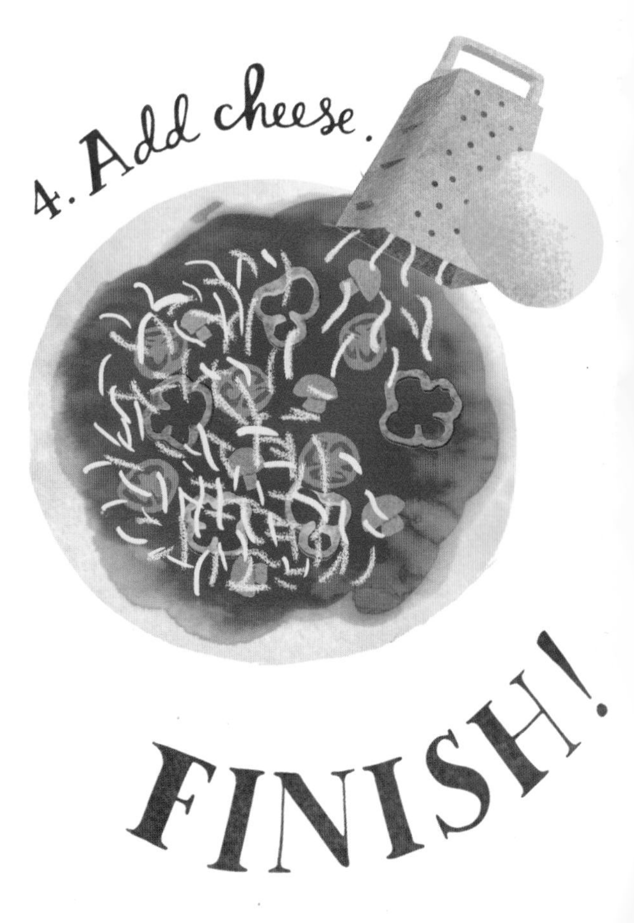

Then we set it in the oven and wait.

While the pizza bakes, we put away our gardening tools and toys.

We brush the wild beast and give him fresh water.

Soon, it's time to eat pizza!

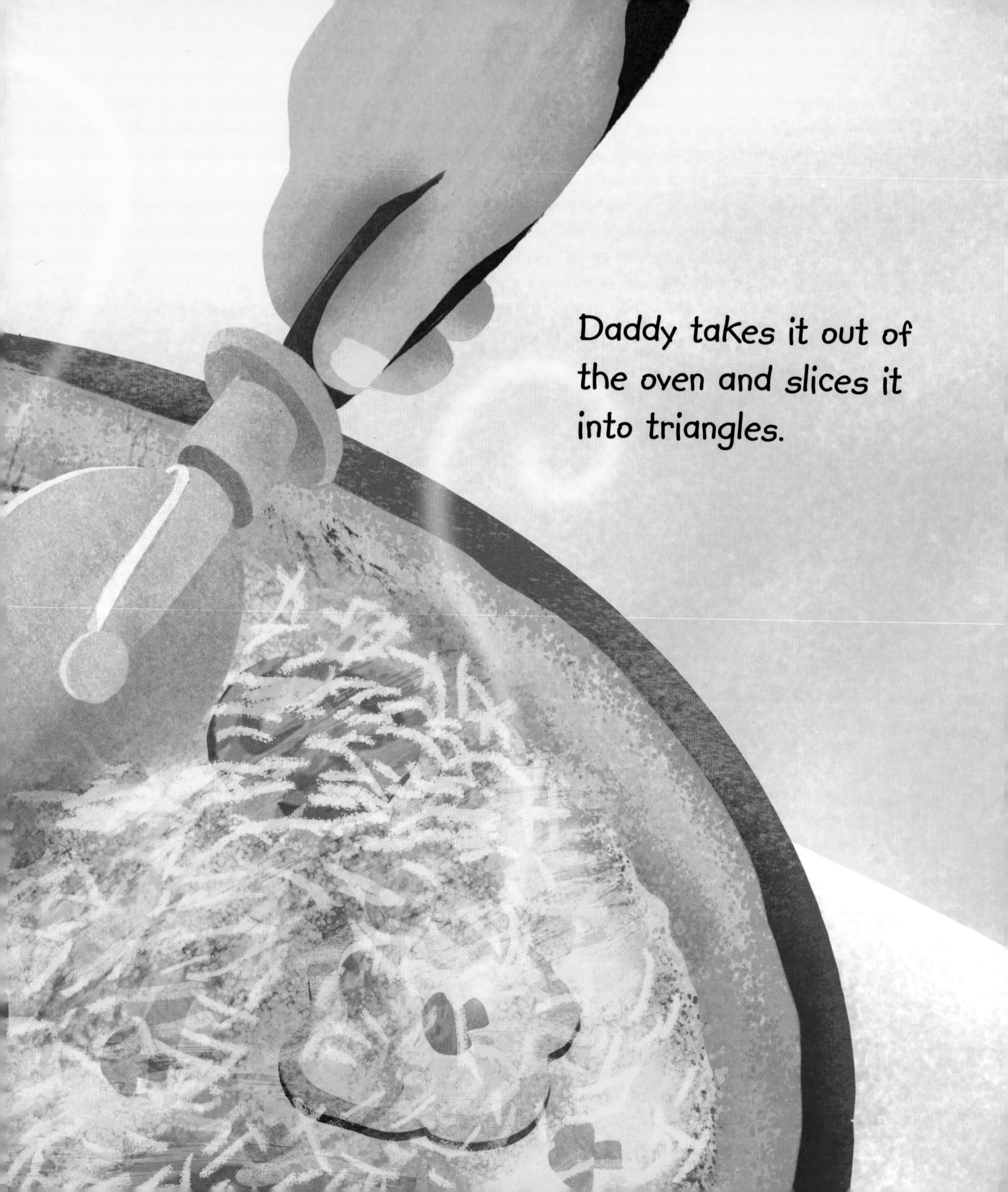

Daddy takes it out of
the oven and slices it
into triangles.

I put a few
basil leaves
on my slice . . .

and take a big bite.

Mmmmmm . . .
I love pizza day.

GARDEN PIZZA

Makes 2 medium pizzas.

Pizza Dough

nonstick spray or oil for greasing

1½ teaspoons active dry yeast

1 cup warm water

2 tablespoons olive oil

1½ teaspoons kosher salt

3 cups flour, divided, plus more if needed

Pizza Sauce

1 tablespoon olive oil

½ cup chopped onion

¼ cup chopped carrot

1½ tablespoons chopped garlic, about 2 cloves

½ teaspoon kosher salt

1 teaspoon dried oregano

1 teaspoon dried basil

2½ cups chopped vine-ripened tomatoes, about 3 large

¼ cup tomato paste

1. Spray a large bowl with nonstick spray. Set aside.
2. Whisk together yeast, water, olive oil, and salt in another large bowl until combined. Let sit for about 5 minutes.
3. Add 2 cups of the flour and mix together until well blended.
4. Add small amounts of the leftover flour gradually (you may use half or all) until dough forms a ball.
5. Sprinkle flour onto a large board or countertop, and dump out dough. Knead for 5 minutes, adding a bit of the remaining flour each time it starts to feel sticky. You want to end up with a smooth, elastic mound of dough.
6. Shape dough into a large ball. Place in the greased bowl and turn the dough to coat it with oil. Cover with a damp cloth and let rest for 1 hour.
7. Heat olive oil in a skillet over medium heat and sauté onions, carrots, garlic, salt, and herbs until onion is translucent.
8. Add tomatoes and paste. Simmer until softened on very low heat, covered, about 20 to 30 minutes. Stir occasionally.
9. Pulse in blender or food processor to desired chunkiness.

Assemble Pizza

1. Preheat oven to 450 degrees for 10 minutes.
2. Divide pizza dough in half and roll each into a ball. Let rest 10 to 15 minutes.
3. Lightly dust 2 baking sheets and a rolling pin with flour. Roll out each ball of dough into a circle on each baking sheet.
4. Use a spoon to spread pizza sauce onto each. Add fresh veggies, pepperoni, cooked sausage, shredded mozzarella, grated parmesan cheese, goat cheese—whatever you like!
5. Bake for 10 to 13 minutes, depending on how crunchy you like your crust.

Note: Please take care to keep children at a distance from burners on the stove.

Anatomy of Pizza

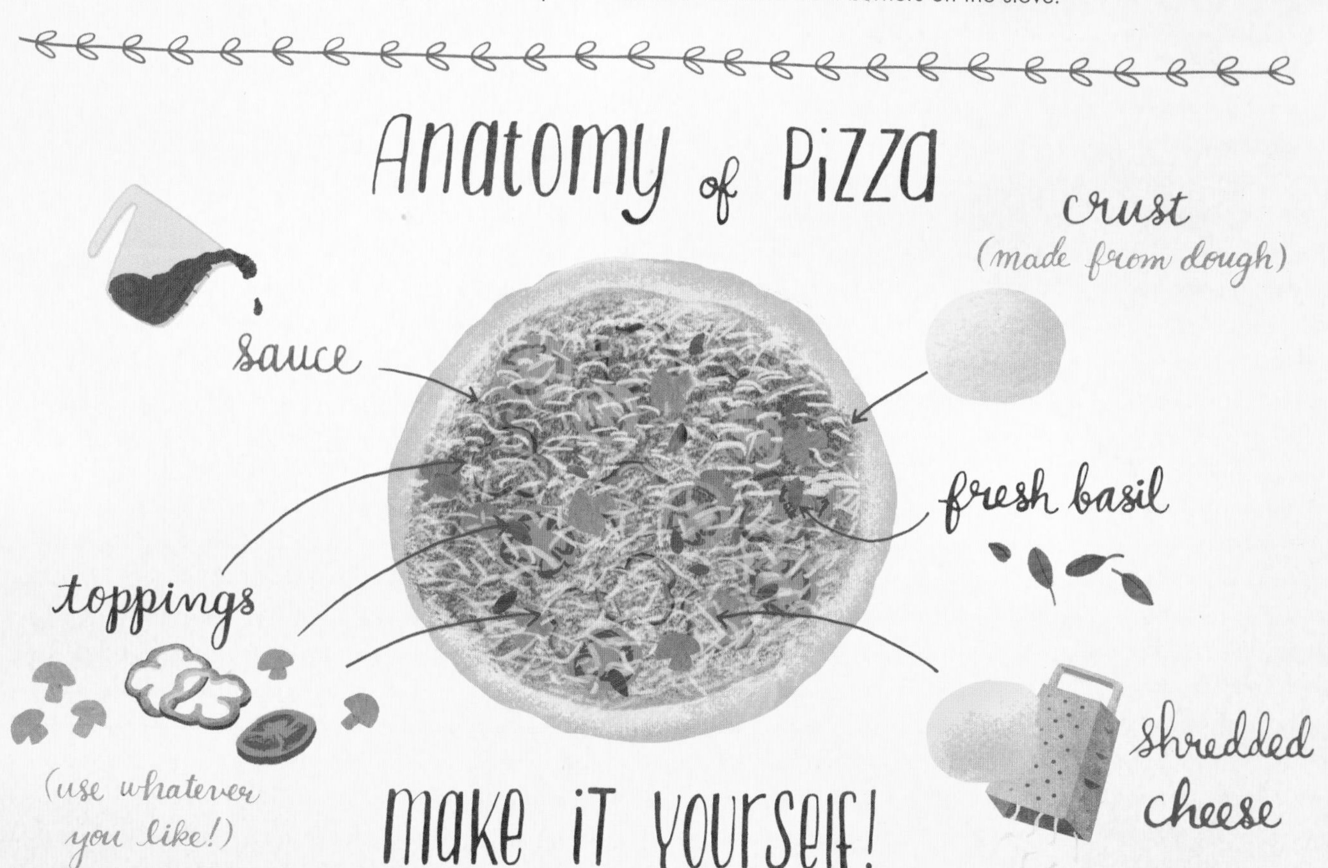

make it yourself!